This Walker book belongs to:

_____

_____

_____

For Sophie – J.E.

For Millie and George, love Auntie Vanessa – V.C.

First published 2011 by Walker Books Ltd
87 Vauxhall Walk, London SE11 5HJ

This edition published 2017

2 4 6 8 10 9 7 5 3 1

Text © 2011 Jonathan Emmett
Illustrations © 2011 Vanessa Cabban

The right of Jonathan Emmett and Vanessa Cabban
to be identified as author and illustrator respectively
of this work has been asserted by them
in accordance with the Copyright, Designs and
Patents Act 1988

This book has been typeset in Beta Bold

Printed in China

British Library Cataloguing in Publication Data:
a catalogue record for this book is available
from the British Library

ISBN 978-1-4063-7324-0

You can find out more about Jonathan Emmett's books
by visiting his website at www.scribblestreet.co.uk

www.walker.co.uk

WALKER BOOKS
AND SUBSIDIARIES
LONDON • BOSTON • SYDNEY • AUCKLAND

A Secret Worth Sharing

Jonathan Emmett

illustrated by
Vanessa Cabban

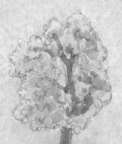

It was a beautiful summer day
in the woodland.
The birds were singing,
the bees were buzzing,
and the sun hung high in the sky,
like a bright golden coin.

"The perfect day to go exploring!"
decided Mole.
And he set off to see
what he could find.

Mole was not used
to being above ground
in warm weather
and so, after a while,
he had to stop for a rest.

"Hot-diggerty!"
he puffed, sitting
down against the side
of a mossy stump.

"Bugs and beetles!"
said a squeaky voice.
"Whatever's that?"

Mole jumped up in surprise
and found a small furry
face peering at him through
a hole in the stump.

"Hello!" he said
nervously. "I'm Mole!
Who are you?"

"I'm Mouse!" said the
face, and gave Mole
the sweetest smile
he had ever seen.

The stump was hollow and Mouse had a nest
inside it. It was a very nice nest,
as Mole discovered when Mouse
invited him in.

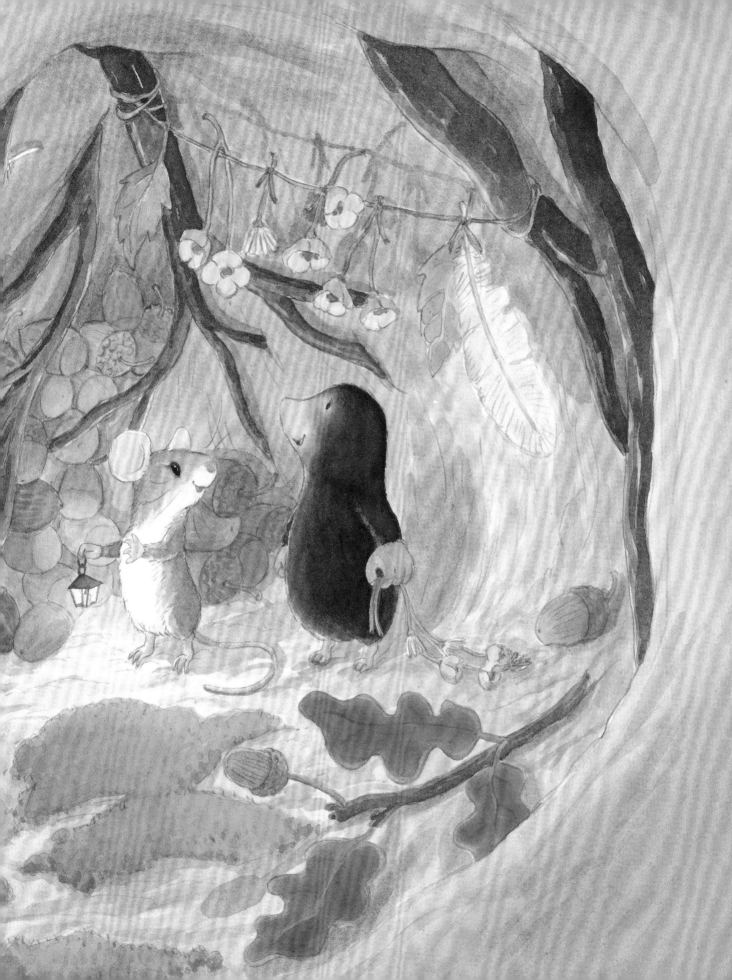

Mole decided that Mouse was very nice too,
and as he walked home that evening,
he felt very pleased with himself
for having made a new friend.
   Mole had other friends, but they all knew
each other. Now he had a friend
all of his own.

"Mouse is my special friend,"
he told himself. And he decided
to keep Mouse a secret and not to tell
anyone about her.

Mole had never had a secret before. It was very exciting and he found it hard to think of anything else.

So he visited Mouse again the next day ...

and the day
after ...

and the day
after that!

Mole spent so much time with Mouse that he didn't
have time for his other friends. Squirrel, Hedgehog
and Rabbit all called round to see Mole,
but he was never in his burrow!

"Where is he?" wondered Squirrel.

"And what's he up to?" wondered Hedgehog.

"I hope he's all right," said Rabbit.

One morning – just as Mole
was hurrying off for another secret visit
to Mouse – Rabbit, Hedgehog and Squirrel arrived.

"Hello, Mole!" said Rabbit. "We haven't seen
much of you recently, so we thought
we'd all pop round."

Mole was disappointed at first. He wanted
to see Mouse again, but he couldn't
tell his friends to go away.

However, once they got talking,
he found himself enjoying their company
as he always did.

"So, Mole," said Rabbit eventually,
"what have you been up to?"

Mole suddenly felt very embarrassed.
"I don't know what you mean," he said.
"I've only –"
But before he could finish,
he was interrupted.

"Hello, Mole! Are you down there?"
called a voice from outside.

It was Mouse!
"I thought I might come and visit
you for a change!"
she explained to Mole.

Rabbit, Hedgehog and Squirrel were very
surprised – but delighted – to meet her,
and Mouse soon made friends with all of them.
But Mole looked rather unhappy.

"What's wrong, Mole?"
asked Rabbit.

"Mouse was my special friend," said Mole glumly,
"but now I'll have to share her with everyone else!"

"But, Mole," said Mouse, giving Mole a hug,
"I'm just as much your friend as ever!
Only now I'm Rabbit's and Squirrel's
and Hedgehog's friend too!"

"Friendship is a very special thing," explained Rabbit, "but one of the things that makes it so special is that the more you share it the more you have!"

"I didn't know that," said Mole.

"So you were keeping me a secret?" smiled Mouse.

Mole blushed. "I suppose I was," he admitted.
"But now I know better.
You're a secret worth SHARING!"
beamed Mole.

Other books by Jonathan Emmett and Vanessa Cabban

ISBN 987-1-4063-7304-2   ISBN 978-1-4063-7311-0

ISBN 978-1-4063-7324-0   ISBN 978-1-4063-7354-7   ISBN 978-1-4063-7353-0

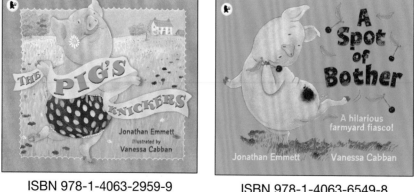

ISBN 978-1-4063-2959-9   ISBN 978-1-4063-6549-8

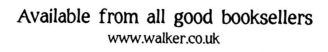

Available from all good booksellers

www.walker.co.uk